Put Beginning Readers on the Right Track with
ALL ABOARD READING™

The All Aboard Reading series is especially designed for beginning readers. Written by noted authors and illustrated in full color, these are books that children really want to read—books to excite their imagination, expand their interests, make them laugh, and support their feelings. With fiction and nonfiction stories that are high interest and curriculum-related, All Aboard Reading books offer something for every young reader. And with four different reading levels, the All Aboard Reading series lets you choose which books are most appropriate for your children and their growing abilities.

Picture Readers
Picture Readers have super-simple texts, with many nouns appearing as rebus pictures. At the end of each book are 24 flash cards—on one side is a rebus picture; on the other side is the written-out word.

Station Stop 1
Station Stop 1 books are best for children who have just begun to read. Simple words and big type make these early reading experiences more comfortable. Picture clues help children to figure out the words on the page. Lots of repetition throughout the text helps children to predict the next word or phrase—an essential step in developing word recognition.

Station Stop 2
Station Stop 2 books are written specifically for children who are reading with help. Short sentences make it easier for early readers to understand what they are reading. Simple plots and simple dialogue help children with reading comprehension.

Station Stop 3
Station Stop 3 books are perfect for children who are reading alone. With longer text and harder words, these books appeal to children who have mastered basic reading skills. More complex stories captivate children who are ready for more challenging books.

In addition to All Aboard Reading books, look for All Aboard Math Readers™ (fiction stories that teach math concepts children are learning in school) and All Aboard Science Readers™ (nonfiction books that explore the most fascinating science topics in age-appropriate language).

All Aboard for happy reading!

D0357696

For Sam who is starting
Kindergarten—G.H.

To Joy—N.G.

Text copyright © 2001 by Gail Herman. Illustrations copyright © 2001 by Norman Gorbaty. All rights reserved. Published by Grosset & Dunlap, a division of Penguin Putnam Books for Young Readers, 345 Hudson Street, New York, NY 10014. ALL ABOARD READING and GROSSET & DUNLAP are trademarks of Penguin Putnam Inc. Published simultaneously in Canada. Printed in the U.S.A.

Library of Congress Control Number: 2001270031

ISBN 0-448-42498-3   K L M N O P Q R S T

All Aboard Reading™

Station Stop
1

Lucky Goes to School!

By Gail Herman
Illustrated by Norman Gorbaty

Grosset & Dunlap • New York

Lucky wakes up.

Something is new today.

Something is different.

"Hurry up, Lucky,"
his boy tells him.
"Today is the first day
of school."

8

Lucky is sad.

What will Lucky do all day?

"Come, Lucky,"
says his boy.
"You can walk
to school
with me."

Lucky and his boy
go down the street.

Now they are at school.

"Good boy,"

says his boy.

He hugs Lucky.

"I will see you soon."

Lucky does not think
he can have fun without his boy.

17

Lucky sees lots of boys and girls.
Lucky sees lots of dogs.
"Good-bye," say the kids.
The dogs wag their tails
but they look sad, too.

Lucky goes to the park.

There are the other dogs.

Lucky wags his tail.

He wants the other dogs

to play with him.

All the dogs wag their tails.
Yes! They do want to play.

The dogs play
"pass the stick."

They chase each other.

They have a snack.

They splash in the mud
and make paw print pictures.

Then they have a nap.
Lucky thinks about his boy.
What is he doing?
Lucky hopes his boy
is having fun at school.

Now it is time to go.

Lucky wags his tail again.
He is saying good-bye
to his new friends.

Lucky goes back to school.

He is with his boy again.

Lucky and his boy walk home.
They are happy.
Tomorrow is another
day of school.